A Message From The Author's Heart

Hello, my name is Lara York and along with my husband Jason, I live in Kennesaw, Georgia where we are Associate and Children's Pastors. We believe the Lord gave this book as a powerful tool for many to come to know Jesus as their loving Lord and Savior, just as we do. We both came to know the Lord at a very young age. For over two decades we have been ministering to children. Our passion is for children and their families to fall in love with Jesus, Father God and His precious Holy Spirit. Our heart is to travel to the nations sharing the love and good news of Jesus with all. A translation of this book is already being worked on for the people of Costa Rica. Our children are the ones we take into our hearts each time we teach them. As well, we have 9 nephews and 5 nieces who bring us much joy. Enjoying life with us are our two wonder dogs, Raya and Porter.

We are grateful for your prayer support over the work and outreach of this book, including those you will take it to. May God's love and blessings be abundant daily in your life and may the harvest be brought in!

He who wins souls is wise. Proverbs 11:30b NIV

About the Artist

Curt Walstead grew up in the small rural community of Merced located in central California. After initially receiving a degree in biology, he redirected his attention to art and earned another degree in illustration from Art Center College of Design. He currently resides with his family near Los Angeles, California where he has worked as an animation storyboard artist and illustrator for over twenty years. During that time he had the opportunity to work on many of today's popular children's shows such as Dragon Tales, Baby Looney Tunes, Clifford's Puppy Days, Dora The Explorer, and Go Diego Go. He has illustrated a number of children's books for numerous publications.

This Book is Dedicated to...

This book is dedicated to the people who shared Jesus with me early in my life, my mother and father, Danny & Gwen Griffin. Also to those who gave me a spiritual heritage, my grandparents, Clifford and Faye Farrar. And to my grandmothers, Lorene Griffin and Faye Farrar for their kind hearts and love for children. May your heart find joy in your eternal reward. I love you all.

It is with deepest gratitude that I offer thanks to Jesus, my Lord and Savior for giving me this opportunity to share His love and goodness with multitudes. To my family for surrounding me with love and support. To everyone who's helped make this a reality from the youngest to the oldest. May you all find great joy in knowing you had a part in reaching each one who comes to know Jesus as Lord through this book.

Text Copyright ©2008 Lara York
Illustration Copyright ©2008 Lara York
Edited by Chris Maiocco and Jon Maiocco
Designed by Tom Cox
All rights reserved.
Published in the United States of America by His Kids Publishing, Inc.,
P.O. Box 72172, Marietta, GA 30007
Printed in China.

For more information about this book, please visit www.zoesgarden.org

How Miss Ladybug Lost Her Spots

by **Lara York**
Illustrated by Curt Walstead

HIS KIDS
PUBLISHING, INC.

hiskidspublishing.com

It was a warm spring day
in the lovely month of May,
Zoe's garden was peacefully at rest,
with baby birds nestled safe in their nest.

Flowers of purple, orange, yellow, and red,
gave beauty and color to each flowerbed.

A crystal clear brook winding and running through
brought water to the flowers and birds and little bugs too.

2

The only movement at all
was a light spring breeze,
gently swaying the flowers
and leaves on the trees.

Nothing could disturb
this warm quiet day,
or so it certainly
seemed that way.

On a sunflower, golden and growing up high,
boldly and beautifully reaching to the sky,
a pretty little ladybug was quietly napping.
She seemed quite calm and even so happy.

Miss Ladybug was quite
different than most,
for in her ladybug spots
she found reason to boast.

Each perfectly round spot
gave her such pride,
but also an attitude,
somewhat snooty and snide.

You see, Miss Ladybug,
southern by birth,
felt that her perfect spots
gave her much worth.

5

The quiet calm of the garden was suddenly gone,
for in came the sounds of laughter and song.

This noise woke Miss Ladybug,
startled and shaken.
She could not believe
she was so rudely awakened.

Miss Ladybug sat up
and thought, "How rude!"
And my, did she ever
have a bad attitude.

6

The laughter and song that caused Miss Ladybug's strife,
came from Zoe, a young girl, who was so full of life.

Zoe was gleeful, singing her song,
jumping and laughing and twirling along.

She always came to this garden, you see,
for her father created it for her, especially.

Seeing the new little Ladybug who had come,
Zoe stopped to meet her and say 'Welcome.'

But before Zoe could speak a single word,
Miss Ladybug harshly snipped,
"Your noisiness is quite absurd!"

8

Knowing this ladybug was new to her garden,
Zoe kindly said, "I apologize and ask for your pardon."

"You should have looked," snapped Miss Ladybug, "and seen I was there,
then you might have taken a little more care."

9

Zoe was kind in every word that she said,
letting love come from her heart,
not mean words from her head.

"I did not see you, or know you were at rest,
I did not mean to be rude or even a pest."

Zoe continued to share such a wonderful love,
the unfailing kind that comes from God above.

Miss Ladybug was surprised at Zoe, being so calm and kind,
for she truly expected her to sharply speak her mind.

This love that Zoe showed was starting to tug,
it was melting the hard heart in Miss Ladybug.

"How is it you are so kind and loving to me?"
Miss Ladybug wanted to know how this could be.

Zoe smiled and gently laughed for now she could say,
"Jesus came into my heart and He made me that way.

"It's Jesus," said Zoe, "He is my Lord and my friend.
His love is so good! Oh, where do I begin?"

13

"Jesus lives in my heart and His love does too.
He's God's only Son who died but now lives for me and you.

"His love He's placed in me is so very real.
It gives me strength to do good
no matter how I feel."

14

Miss Ladybug wondered, "Is it real, such a powerful love?
If so, it could only come from God above."

So humbly she asked, "Can I know this love too?
It is so powerful and kind, so pure and true."

15

"Oh yes," said Zoe, her heart filled with great joy.
"Jesus' love is for you and me, and every girl and boy.

"I will tell you all Jesus did,
He wants us all to be free.
He came to this earth
to live and die for you and me."

16

"He died?" asked Miss Ladybug, "I don't understand.
If He is not living, how can I ever know this man?"

"Yes, He died," answered Zoe, "but that's not the end.
God had a plan for His Son, Jesus, to soon live again."

17

"He died for all we've done
wrong and He paid the price.
His pure and perfect life
became our sin's sacrifice.

"Then after three days,
He rose from His grave,
and gave us all a great gift,
for our lives He did save.

"God gave everything to save us
when He gave Jesus, His only Son.
He knew there was no other way
this could ever be done.

"God loves us all so dearly.
He made heaven for our eternity.
When we receive Jesus in our heart,
He brings us into His family."

"Is it true?" asked Miss Ladybug,
"I too can be forgiven?
What Jesus did is the way
to have a life worth living?"

"Certainly, Miss Ladybug,"
Zoe was glad to say.
"I will tell you how to start
your brand new life today."

19

"To receive Jesus as your Savior, believe in all He did and said.
In your heart believe He is God's Son, who is raised from the dead.

"Ask God to forgive you for all the wrong you've ever done,
knowing you will be forever changed by His precious Son.

"Then say out loud for all to know and hear,
'Jesus, I trust and receive You as my Lord
and Savior and that will make it clear."

Miss Ladybug knew she wanted Jesus in her heart,
and now she understood she had to do her part.
She believed the wonderful good news Zoe had proclaimed,
knowing the love she'd seen could not otherwise be explained.

She said these words out loud, and did not just think them in her head,
"Jesus, You are the Son of God, who He raised from the dead.
I ask you to be my Savior, and I receive all you have done.
I'm so thankful God has given His one and only Son.

"Because you are my Lord and Savior, You now live inside of me.
I will love You, know You, and serve You, and share your love so free."

22

"Miss Ladybug," Zoe exclaimed, "for you this is such a happy day. Jesus has made you new inside, and now the old you has gone away.

"Now that He is in your heart, you have His loves' power, too. You can be loving, kind and gentle in all you say and do."

23

Tears of joy trickled down
Miss Ladybug's sweet little face.
Jesus came into her heart.
Love had taken meanness' place.

"I have to say I'm sorry for
how rude I was before."
Zoe accepted her apology saying,
"I'll remember it no more."

24

"Look," exclaimed Zoe, "something is happening to you!
Your spots are disappearing and now there's something new."

"Oh my," squealed Miss Ladybug. "My old spots are gone, I see.
Jesus changed my spots to hearts to show just what He did in me."

"You're right," said Zoe, "and I think you should have a new name.
Miss Lovebug suits you now, for you will never be the same."

"It's a wonderful name," said Miss Lovebug, "and it will help all to see
since Jesus now lives in my heart, there truly is a brand new me!"

"Miss Lovebug?" asked Zoe, "I know I've met you just today, but I'd like to invite you to live here in my garden to stay."

"Oh yes," answered Miss Lovebug, "you are a real friend, it's true. You have kindly led me to Jesus, I'd love to stay with you."

From that day on Miss Lovebug lived happily in the garden of her new friend. Many adventures were yet to come, but as for this one, that's *The End*.

This story tells a very important truth. God really sent His only Son, Jesus, to earth to live as a man. He lived a perfect life so His death on the cross would be a pure sacrifice for the sin of everyone. By realizing we have all sinned, asking for forgiveness, trusting Jesus, and receiving Him as our Lord and Savior, we are saved from the punishment of our sin. All wrongdoing is sin and separates us from God. Through Jesus we are made brand new and become God's child, just as He always wanted.

To find out more, read the following Bible verses. (Note: All scripture below is from the New Living Translation.)

Romans 3:23 "For everyone has sinned; we all fall short of God's glorious standard."

John 3:16 "For God loved the world so much that He gave his one and only Son, so that everyone who believes in Him will not perish but have eternal life."

John 14:6 Jesus told him, "I am the way, the truth, and the life. No one can come to the Father except through me."

Romans 10:9-10 "If you confess with your mouth that Jesus is Lord and believe in your heart that God raised Him from the dead, you will be saved. For it is by believing in your heart that you are made right with God, and it is by confessing with your mouth that you are saved."

Acts 4:12 "There is salvation in no one else! God has given no other name under heaven by which we must be saved."

Romans 10:13 "Everyone who calls on the name of the Lord will be saved."

Romans 5:5 "And this hope will not lead to disappointment. For we know how dearly God loves us, because he has given us the Holy Spirit to fill our hearts with his love."

John 1:12 "But to all who believed Him and accepted Him, He gave the right to become children of God."

2 Corinthians 5:17 "This means that anyone who belongs to Christ has become a new person. The old life is gone; a new life has begun!"

If you would like to ask Jesus to be the Lord and Savior of your life, please say the following prayer, believing it in your heart; then tell someone of your decision.

Dear God, I know I am a sinner and I need a Savior. You said in Your Word, if I confess with my mouth Jesus is Lord and believe in my heart You raised Him from the dead, I will be saved. I believe Jesus is Lord and that You raised Him from the dead. I believe He died on the cross to pay for my sins. I ask you to forgive me and make me new. Jesus, I ask you to come into my heart and be my Savior and the Lord of my life.

If you prayed this prayer to make Jesus the Lord & Savior of your life or would like to know more about being a Christian, please contact us by email at myfaithchurch@bellsouth.net or by mail at Faith Church, ATTN:Pastor, PO Box 1537, Kennesaw, GA 30156. We want to rejoice with you and send you a free gift for your new life as a Christian. God loves you and we do too!

FAITH CHURCH OF KENNESAW, GA